Parent's Introduction

Whether your child is a beginning reader, a reluctant reader, or an eager reader, this book offers a fun and easy way to encourage and help your child in reading.

Developed with reading education specialists, *We Both Read* books invite you and your child to take turns reading aloud. You read the left-hand pages of the book, and your child reads the right-hand pages—which have been written at one of six early reading levels. The result is a wonderful new reading experience and faster reading development!

You may find it helpful to read the entire book aloud yourself the first time, then invite your child to participate the second time. As you read, try to make the story come alive by reading with expression. This will help to model good fluency. It will also be helpful to stop at various points to discuss what you are reading. This will help increase your child's understanding of what is being read.

In some books, a few challenging words are introduced in the parent's text, distinguished with **bold** lettering. Pointing out and discussing these words can help to build your child's reading vocabulary. If your child is a beginning reader, it may be helpful to run a finger under the text as each of you reads. Please also notice that a "talking parent" ☺ icon precedes the parent's text, and a "talking child" ☺ icon precedes the child's text.

If your child struggles with a word, you can encourage "sounding it out," but keep in mind that not all words can be sounded out. Your child might pick up clues about a word from the picture, other words in the sentence, or any rhyming patterns. If your child struggles with a word for more than five seconds, it is usually best to simply say the word.

Most of all, remember to praise your child's efforts and keep the reading fun. After you have finished the book, ask a few questions and discuss what you have read together. Rereading this book multiple times may also be helpful for your child.

Try to keep the tips above in mind as you read together, but don't worry about doing everything right. Simply sharing the enjoyment of reading together will increase your child's reading skills and help to start your child off on a lifetime of reading enjoyment!

We Both Read: My Sitter Is a T-Rex!

Text Copyright © 2011 by Paul Orshoski
Illustrations Copyright © 2011 by Jeffrey Ebbeler

We Both Read® is a trademark of Treasure Bay, Inc.

Published by
Treasure Bay, Inc.
P. O. Box 119
Novato, CA 94948 USA

Printed in Singapore

Library of Congress Catalog Card Number: 2010932587

Hardcover ISBN-13: 978-1-60115-253-4
Paperback ISBN-13: 978-1-60115-254-1

We Both Read® Books
Patent No. 5,957,693

Visit us online at:
www.WeBothRead.com

PR 11/10

WE BOTH READ®

My Sitter
Is a T-Rex!

By Paul Orshoski

Illustrated by Jeffrey Ebbeler

TREASURE BAY

My parents have a date tonight. They're going to a show.
I ask them, "Who will babysit?" Mom says she doesn't know.

She says, "I called an agency."

 "I called them rather late.

They only had one sitter left.

I'm sure she will be great."

The doorbell rings. Mom lets her in. I stare with great surprise.
A dinosaur is at my door. I can't believe my eyes.

She says, "I'm here to babysit. That's what I plan to do.
Most people call me Miss T-Rex, but you can call me Sue."

4

I hide in back of Mom and Dad.

My legs begin to shake.

I beg them, "Please, you cannot leave.

There must be some mistake."

 But Dad says, "Don't you worry, Todd. I'm sure she is a jewel. We really have to say **goodbye**." Then Sue begins to drool.

I see her teeth and two short arms.

I soon begin to cry.

But Mom and Dad fly out the door.

Miss T-Rex waves **goodbye**.

7

 I run for cover to my room. I scream and race to hide.
I sneak behind a chest of drawers. My fear is deep and wide.

And soon I'm underneath my bed.

I'm too afraid to peek.

Sue spots me and says, "Peek-a-boo.

Let's play some hide and seek." 9

I dash away. Sue counts to ten. My legs are feeling numb.
Then Sue roars loudly, "Ready, Todd? Okay, then, here I come!"

I try to hide as best I can. I'm scared more than before.
"Please go away," I say to Sue. She sits down on the floor.

 "Come out and say hello to me."

Miss T-Rex sounds so sweet.

"You do not wish to come and play?

Then I will go and eat."

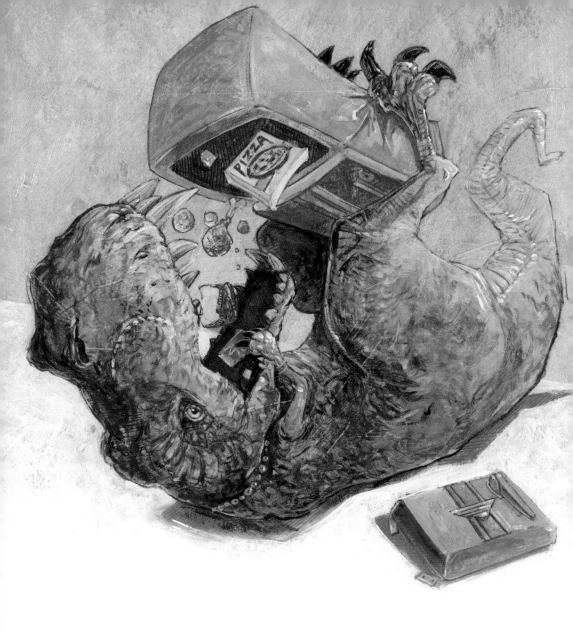

So Sue begins to hunt for food. I give a careful stare.
She opens up the freezer door and flings it through the air.

She grabs a drumstick from the fridge. She stuffs it in her face.
She picks up every speck of food and empties out the place!

She pours a cup of purple punch.

She grabs a slab of pie.

She slips and trips on Mom's new rug.

I see the cup fly by!

Sue wanders to the living room. Her food is stacked up **high**. I sneak around to take a peek as Sue goes stomping by.

Her tail rips all the curtains down. A lamp gets shattered too. She **breaks** a pretty flower vase. Oh no! That vase was new!

She lumbers past the TV set.

The room begins to shake.

A clock **high** on the wall falls down.

I see it smash and **break**.

Sue shuffles to an easy chair. She sits and rests her feet.
She grabs my dad's remote control and eats another treat.

I see the chair begin to sway. I hear it creak and groan!
She dumps her purse out on the floor so she can find her phone.

Sue sends a text to all her friends.
They text her back. She grins.
She laughs so hard she starts to snort.
And in the chair she spins.

Sue gets up from her easy chair. She says, "I think I'll read."
She searches through the shelves of books for one she just
might need.

She spots a book on outer space and one about a clown.

Sue takes a book from way on top.

Then all the books fall down.

Sue walks back through the kitchen door. Her tummy needs more food.
She quickly chugs a soda down. She belches loud. How rude!

She chews a wad of bubble gum. I cannot help but stare.
She blows a great big bubble. **POP!** Now gum is EVERYWHERE!

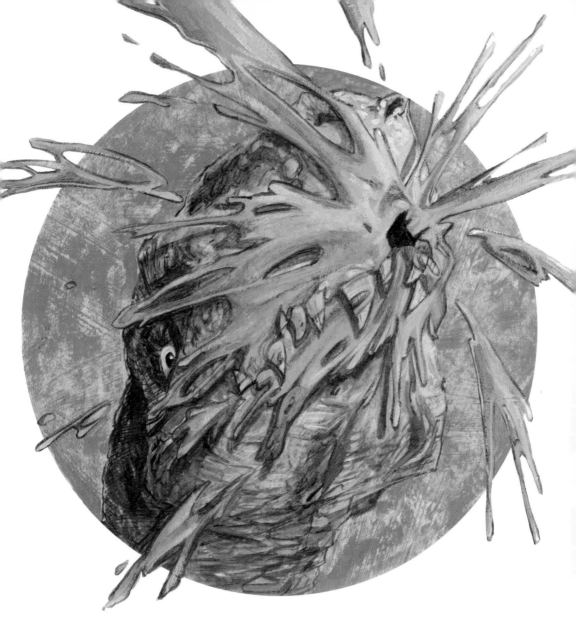

The gum is on her nose and lips.

It's on her cheek and chin.

It's in her tail. It's on her feet.

It's on her spine and skin.

The gum is sticking to the rug. It's sticking to my hair! **There's** some stuck on the window pane. **There's** some stuck to the chair.

The ceiling also has some gum.

And so does Mom's clean floor.

There's some stuck on the table top.

There's some stuck on the door.

By now I've had enough of this! I storm in raving mad!
When Mom comes home and sees this mess, it's going
to make her sad.

My dad will be unhappy too. His patience is quite thin.
I turn to Sue and yell at her, "Why did we let you in!?"

 " You broke my mother's flower vase.

You filled me up with fear.

You ate our food and made a mess.

I wish you were not here!"

Sue looks surprised by what I said.
She hangs her **head** down low.
Her lips begin to tremble.
And her tears begin to flow.

She lifts her **head** and looks at me.

Her eyes are big and sad.

She says, "I'm sorry for this mess.

And that I made you mad."

 "I tried to do my very best.
I did not want to fail.
Now I'll clean up the mess I've made.
I'll get a mop and pail."

I feel so bad that Sue is sad.

Perhaps I was too mean.

I scale Sue's neck and hug her close.

I say, "I'll help you clean."

We go to work together now to fix the vase and clock.
We also fix the broken lamp while chanting, "Tick, tick, tock."

We put the curtains back in place, the clock back on the wall.

We have a few things yet to do.

At least I hope that's all!

We go into the kitchen next to fix the freezer door.
I have some screws and handy tools. Sue lifts me off the floor.

We grab some soap and two big pails, a scraper, and a mop.

We scrape and clean the sticky mess.

My home is rid of slop!

Sue says, "I'm feeling hungry now. I'd love a chicken wing!"
I laugh out loud and say to Sue, "You ate up everything!"

She laughs with me and then we hug. I stick to her like glue.

So then I send Sue to the tub.

She needs some cleaning too.

The tub is full. Sue squeezes in. The rubber duck says, "Quack." Sue scrubs her face and then calls out, "Please, Todd, come wash my back."

I close my eyes. I grab a **towel**.

I soap her back quite well.

Sue hops on out and **towels** right off.

She says, "I feel just swell."

We find some pillows and a quilt. We sit down on the floor. I start to read a book to Sue. And then I hear her snore.

I leave her sleeping peacefully.

 I kiss her on the cheek.

I hope I do not wake her up.

Then to my bed I sneak.

When Mom and Dad at last come home, Mom asks, "How did it go?
Did you both get along okay? I'd really like to know."

"I haven't had such fun," I say, "since can't remember when."

I wave at Sue and say to Mom,

"I want Sue back again!"

41

If you liked *My Sitter Is a T-Rex!*, here is another
We Both Read® book you are sure to enjoy!

Baseball Fever

This is a humorous book about something everyone has experienced—being sick! When Jason gets sick, he is told that he has to stay home and get better. But he is supposed to pitch in an important game in a few days! While Jason is doing his best to get better, he learns that being sick is easiest to face with the support of family and friends.

To see all the We Both Read books that are available,
just go online to **www.WeBothRead.com**.